"This is a job for the T.C.D.C.," Timothy told Sarah-Jane and Titus. "First the ring gets lost. And now someone bursts the balloons on the car."

"Whoever it was got clean away," said Titus. Suddenly he called, "Hey, you guys! Come here QUICK!"

THE MYSTERY OF THE
MESSED-UP WEDDING

Elspeth Campbell Murphy
Illustrated by Chris Wold Dyrud

Chariot Books
David C. Cook Publishing Co.

A Wise Owl Book
Published by Chariot Books,
an imprint of David C. Cook Publishing Co.
David C. Cook Publishing Co., Elgin, Illinois 60120
David C. Cook Publishing Co., Weston, Ontario

The Mystery of the Messed-up Wedding
© 1988 by Elspeth Campbell Murphy for text and Chris Wold
Dyrud for illustrations

Cover design by Chris Patchel
First Printing, 1988
Printed in the United States of America
93 92 91 90 89 88 5 4 3 2 1

Library of Congress Cataloging-in-Publication Data
Murphy, Elspeth Campbell.
    The mystery of the messed-up wedding.

    (The Ten Commandments mysteries)
    Summary: While attending a wedding, three cousins solve a
mystery of a lost wedding ring and learn about the commitment
married partners make to each other.
    [1. Cousins—Fiction. 2. Mystery and detective stories. 3. Ten
commandments—Fiction.]
I. Dyrud, Chris Wold, ill. II. Title. III. Series:
Murphy, Elspeth Campbell. Ten Commandments mysteries.
PZ7.M95316Mye   1988   [FIC]   87-16720
ISBN 1-55513-687-7

"You shall not commit adultery."

Exodus 20:14 (NIV)

CONTENTS

1
THE WEDDING DAY

Whenever the cousins Timothy, Titus, and Sarah-Jane stayed with their grandparents, they did two things.

They looked at family photographs with their grandmother. And they said their Bible verses for their grandfather.

They loved to look at pictures of when their mothers were three little sisters growing up together.

But Sarah-Jane's favorites were their mothers' wedding pictures.

There was going to be a wedding that afternoon at the church where Grandpa was the pastor.

All morning long Sarah-Jane had been walking around with an old lace curtain over her head, singing, "Here Comes the Bride."

She sighed happily and said, "Weddings are *so wonderful*! I love the flowers! I love the *beautiful* dresses!"

"Weddings are *weird*, you mean," said Timothy.

"Yeah, weird," said Titus. "Everybody gets nervous and acts crazy."

Grandpa laughed. "You're both right," he said. "Weddings *are* wonderful. But people *do* get a little weird if everything doesn't go exactly right. That's why they're so lucky to have your grandma."

It was true. The cousins' grandfather, Pastor Gordon, performed the ceremony. But it was Mrs. Gordon, their grandmother, who made things go smoothly. She knew everything there was to know about weddings. So brides and grooms always came to her for help.

Grandma closed the photograph album. She said, "We'd better have an early lunch today. Christina's and Jerry's wedding is at two o'clock. There will be a lot going on over at the church. The bride and her bridesmaids will be getting dressed there. Also, I have to check on the flowers and the cake."

Titus said, "Jerry's car is all decorated. I saw his friends park it behind the church. It's covered with crepe paper streamers and tissue paper flowers and even balloons!"

Again Sarah-Jane sighed happily. "Jerry will be a handsome groom. Christina will be a *beautiful* bride. And even the car looks wonderful!"

"It looks *weird*, you mean," said Timothy with a grin. Then he pulled off Sarah-Jane's curtain veil and tossed it to Titus. The boys made her chase them to get it back.

Sarah-Jane chased Timothy and Titus all the way across the lawn to the church. They didn't look where they were going. And they bumped into the groom's teenage sister, Jill.

She was carrying a pink dress in a plastic bag in one hand. And she had a box of wedding programs in the other. The programs spilled out all over the lawn.

"Hey! Watch where you're going!" Jill yelled at them.

"Sorry!" the cousins said.

They scooped up the programs and helped Jill put them back into the box.

Sarah-Jane pointed to the dress that Jill was carrying. "Is that your bridesmaid's dress, Jill? Grandma told me Christina's bridesmaids are wearing pink. Pink is my very favorite color!"

Jill rolled her eyes as if Sarah-Jane had asked a really dumb question. "Are you kidding?" she said. "I wouldn't be a bridesmaid if you *paid* me! All I'm going to do is stand at the stupid door and hand out the stupid programs." Then she picked up the box and stomped into the church.

"Wow!" said Sarah-Jane as they walked back

to the house. "She's not exactly the *nicest* person I ever met."

Timothy said, "I'm telling you, it's *weddings*. They make people get nervous and act weird."

"I feel sorry for the guests," said Titus as they climbed the back porch steps. "When Jill meets them at the church door, she'll say, 'Take a program, or I'll knock your block off!' "

2
THE LOST RING

The three cousins bounced into the kitchen.

"Come tell me your Bible verses before lunch," said Grandpa.

This was something the cousins loved to do. They leaned on Grandpa's chair. He put his arms around them and nodded his head as they spoke the words.

Sarah-Jane said the Lord's Prayer. Timothy said the Twenty-third Psalm. Titus said the Ten Commandments.

Titus asked, "Grandpa, you know the part that says, 'You shall not commit adultery'? I don't know what that means."

Grandpa said, "That commandment is a special law for husbands and wives, Titus. When two people get married, they make an important promise to God and to each other. They promise they will love each other—and only each other—in a special way.

"That's why people wear wedding rings. The rings show that the people have made a promise. Adultery is when the promise is broken."

Sarah-Jane said, "I saw Christina's wedding ring. Jerry showed it to me when he came for the rehearsal last night. It's beautiful!"

"It certainly is a beautiful ring," agreed Grandma. "It once belonged to Jerry's great-grandmother."

Just then the back doorbell rang. "Why, Jerry!" said Grandma, opening the door for him. "We were just talking about you, and about the ring you're giving Christina."

"That's what I came to see you about," said Jerry miserably. "The ring is gone!"

"GONE!?" they all cried together.

Then Grandma said, "Let's all be calm about this. Tell us what happened, Jerry. When did you last see the ring?"

"Last night," said Jerry. "I wanted Christina to try it on—the jeweler had fixed it to fit her finger."

He went on, "Anyway, I took the ring out of the little box. I left the box in my jacket pocket. Christina tried on the ring, and it fit just right. Then she gave it back to me."

Grandma asked, "And *then* what did you do, Jerry?"

Jerry frowned, thinking hard. "I put the ring back in the little box in my jacket pocket. . . . At least, I *think* I did. I've been trying and trying to remember exactly. But I can't! Weddings are so busy and confusing.

"Anyway, this morning my best man, Bob, came over to get the ring. The box was still in my jacket pocket. But the box was empty. The ring was gone."

Titus asked, "Do you think a stranger snuck into the church and stole it?"

"Oh, no. I don't think so," said Jerry. "I think someone would have noticed a stranger. And besides, how would the thief have known where to look?

"No, I think I was just absentminded," he went on. "I think I must have set the ring down

16

somewhere and forgot it. Maybe it rolled under a pew. I don't know. But I *do* know that I need help looking for it. Christina and her bridesmaids are too busy getting ready. And besides, I don't want to upset everyone. I just want to find the ring in time for the wedding.''

"You need the T.C.D.C." said Timothy.

"EXcellent idea!" said Titus.

"What's a 'teesy-deesy'?" asked Grandma, Grandpa, and Jerry.

"It's letters," said Sarah-Jane.

"Capital T.

Capital C.
Capital D.
Capital C.
It stands for Three Cousins Detective Club.
Come on, you guys. Let's go find that ring!''

3
THE SEARCH

Timothy, Titus, and Sarah-Jane were sure they would find the ring right away.

They ran next door to the church ahead of their grandparents and Jerry.

The grown-ups and the kids covered all the places Jerry had been the night before. They searched high and low for the ring.

It just wasn't there.

Grandma and Grandpa had a lot of work to do, so they had to leave.

Grandpa said to Jerry, "Don't worry. I'm sure the ring will turn up."

Grandma said, "Jerry, I have a ring you can borrow for the ceremony, if we don't find your own ring in time. But I know how much you want your own. And I'm sure the T.C.D.C. will do their best."

Timothy, Titus, and Sarah-Jane had felt like giving up. But when Grandma said that about the T.C.D.C., they wanted to keep trying.

So they kept looking with Jerry. They crawled under pews. They looked in hymnbook racks. They even got flashlights and peered into the grates on the floor.

But the ring was nowhere to be found.

Finally Jerry had to leave to get ready for the wedding.

"He sure looks sad and worried," said Titus.

"You're right, Ti," said Sarah-Jane. "It's so awful that this happened! Weddings are supposed to be happy."

"Well, let's not give up yet," said Timothy. "We've still got time before the ceremony."

But they didn't have *much* time.

The florist had already finished decorating the sanctuary.

The baker had already set up the cake for the reception in the social hall downstairs.

And the cousins had already searched everywhere they could think of for the ring.

They weren't sure what to do next.

Sarah-Jane stopped to admire the bouquets, corsages, and boutonnieres laid out and waiting.

"I like the kind of flowers you can *eat*!" said Timothy.

So they went to take a peek at the wedding cake. It was beautiful and *big*.

Timothy and Titus counted the big, sugary flowers. They wanted to see how many pieces of cake would have extra frosting.

"I sure hope I get a flower!" said Timothy.

"Me, too," said Titus. "Or at least an edge

21

part."

"Me, too," said Sarah-Jane. But she was really looking at the little bride-and-groom figure on top of the cake.

At last she said, "Well, Tim and Ti. What do we do now?"

The boys shrugged sadly.

All three were quiet, thinking about the missing ring.

They heard music from the sanctuary. The organist was practicing.

They heard the clatter of dishes from the kitchen. Some ladies from the church were getting ready for the reception.

And then from outside they heard bang-bang-bang!

Bang-bang-bang!

Bang-bang-bang-bang-bang!

Timothy, Titus, and Sarah-Jane stared at one another in amazement. Then—all at the same time—they cried, "The balloons!"

4
A FANCY PIN

The cousins dashed out of the social hall, up the stairs, and out into the little driveway behind the church.

It was exactly as they had feared.

Every single balloon on Jerry's car was burst.

All that was left of the balloons were sad, little scraps of pink and white rubber.

"Man, this wedding sure is getting messed up!" said Timothy. "First the ring gets lost. And now someone bursts the balloons."

"Whoever it was got clean away," said Titus.

Sarah-Jane groaned. "The car looked so pretty before. Now it looks just awful."

"It's not *totally* wrecked," said Titus. "The crepe paper and flowers still look OK."

Sarah-Jane brightened up a little. "You're

right, Ti," she said. "At least we could cut off the broken balloons. And while we're doing that, we can keep looking around the car for the ring.

"Jerry's friends started working on the car last night. Maybe Jerry came out here to look at it. Maybe he had the ring and dropped it."

They rushed off to get scissors from their grandmother and to tell her what had happened.

Grandmother listened carefully as they breathlessly told her about the balloons.

"This is very upsetting," she said at last. "I imagine it's some neighborhood kids who did it. But we've never had any trouble like this before. It's too bad if that's their idea of a joke."

She added, "See what you can do to fix up the car. You can get some scissors from a Sunday school room."

Back at the car, Timothy, Titus, and Sarah-Jane carefully snipped off the broken balloons.

Timothy and Sarah-Jane went to throw the scraps away.

Titus started hunting for the ring. Suddenly he called, "Hey, you guys! Come here QUICK!"

"The ring!" cried Timothy, racing over. "You

24

found the ring!''

"Well, not exactly,'' said Titus. "But I *did* find a clue.'' He held out his hand. "I think someone accidentally dropped this. I think this is the *weapon* that burst the balloons!''

"A pin! Of course!'' said Sarah-Jane. "Good work, Ti!''

"It's a really *fancy* pin,'' said Timothy. "Look at this little pearly part on the tip.''

Sarah-Jane said, "This is the kind of pin ladies use to put on a corsage. Or men could use it for a boutonniere.''

Timothy gave a puzzled frown. "But why would the neighborhood kids have a pin like this? Wait a minute! Are you thinking what I'm thinking?"

Titus nodded excitedly. "I think you're onto something, Tim. The balloons were burst *by someone who's part of the wedding*! And here's something else. I don't think Jerry *lost* the ring. I think somebody *took* it!"

"What do you mean?" asked Sarah-Jane. "Jerry said he was *sure* a stranger didn't come in the church last night."

Titus shook his head. "I know that, S-J. But maybe a *stranger* didn't take the ring. Maybe a *friend* took it."

"The same person who burst the balloons?" asked Timothy.

Again Titus shook his head. "I don't know. But you were right, Tim. You said this wedding is getting all messed up. And I think someone is messing it up *on purpose*!"

"What a rotten thing to do!" cried Sarah-Jane. "Weddings are supposed to be wonderful. People make promises to each other. And they give each other rings. Why would anyone want to be SO MEAN and mess things up like this?"

"I don't know," said Titus, as they went to put the scissors away. "Maybe someone is playing a stupid joke and thinks it's funny."

"Or maybe someone's really *mad* about something," said Timothy.

They had just put the scissors into the cabinet when suddenly, from the social hall, there came a scream.

The scream came from one of the reception ladies.

She pointed to the top of the wedding cake. "Look at that! Look at that!" she said to the other ladies and the three cousins. "I just came in here with the punch bowl—and THAT is what I find!"

The cousins saw that the little bride-and-groom figure on top of the cake was turned upside down. Their feet were in the air, and their heads were in the frosting. The cake itself was OK—except for a little smear.

The lady took the figure off the cake to clean it and put it right side up.

Just then an outside door slammed. "Come on!" the cousins said to each other. Someone is getting away!''

They flew down the hallway, up the stairs, and barged out of the door themselves.

They were just in time to see a flash of pink disappear around the corner of the church.

By the time they got to the corner, the person was gone.

"What did I tell you?" said Timothy. "Someone is really trying to mess up this wedding!"

The cousins walked up and down the church sidewalk as they talked about the problem.

Inside the church, the organist started playing the prelude. The wedding would begin in half an hour.

"It's probably one of the bridesmaids," said Titus.

"WHAT?" cried Sarah-Jane indignantly. (She liked bridesmaids almost as much as she liked brides.) "Are you crazy, Ti? If a person's lucky enough to be a bridesmaid, why would she mess up the wedding?"

"Just think about it, S-J," pleaded Titus. "We saw a flash of pink. And you said the bridesmaids' dresses are pink."

"*Lots* of people wear pink to weddings," said Sarah-Jane stubbornly.

"But it couldn't be a guest," said Titus. "The guests are only starting to get here now. All this messing up started when someone took the ring. And it's been going on all afternoon—with the balloons and the cake. *It's got to be someone who's part of the wedding.*"

"Ti's right, S-J," said Timothy. "Remember the pin we found. It must have been a *bridesmaid* who burst the balloons with her corsage pin."

"Aha!" cried Sarah-Jane. "That shows how much *you* know! Bridesmaids don't wear corsages! They carry bouquets—like the bride. So there!"

"Then who were those corsages for?" asked Timothy.

Sarah-Jane cooled down and thought about Timothy's question. "Different people," she said. "The bride's mother gets a corsage. The groom's mother gets one, too. And the grandmothers. And, like, if you have any special helpers at a wedding, they could get corsages, too.''

''What kind of helpers?'' asked Titus.

''It depends,'' said Sarah-Jane. ''It could be a lady who sings a song or reads a poem or passes out programs. . . .''

They had reached the church steps.

Sarah-Jane stopped dead in her tracks.

Timothy and Titus looked at her and said together, ''Jill?''

"I think so," said Sarah-Jane. "Jill told us that she didn't want to be a bridesmaid, remember?

"But I don't think that's true. I think she was *mad* because she didn't get to be one."

Titus said, "So she tried to get even by messing up the wedding?"

Timothy said, "It's like Sarah-Jane said before, Ti. Jill is not exactly the nicest person we ever met. But I think we'd better stop wondering and just ask her for the ring back. The wedding starts in less than half an hour. And Jerry will be here any minute."

They ran lightly up the church steps and slipped through the big front doors.

They saw Jill across the vestibule. She was standing at the door to the sanctuary. A few

33

guests had just gone in, and Jill was alone.

"This isn't going to be easy," whispered Sarah-Jane. "I like it when teenagers are nice. I *don't* like it when they're snotty. Jill will probably tell us to get lost."

"Don't worry," said Timothy. "We have proof. Look at her corsage."

"Yes," said Titus with a grin. "And she's wearing another clue—on her sleeve."

"Well, here goes," said Sarah-Jane.

8
HURRY!

Each cousin took a deep breath. Then together they crossed the vestibule.

"Jill, we need to talk to you about something," said Sarah-Jane all in a rush.

Jill looked at them as if three little cockroaches had crawled out of the wall and said, "Hi, there!"

Several guests came over for programs. Jill waited until the guests were inside. Then she muttered, "What do you want?"

"We need the ring back," said Sarah-Jane.

"I don't know what you're talking about!" said Jill. But she looked very surprised and very upset.

More guests came in.

The cousins were running out of time.

"Your corsage is crooked," said Timothy. "It needs another pin like this." He held out the pearly topped pin.

"Where did you get that?" asked Jill angrily. She started to grab it, but more guests were coming.

When they were gone, Timothy whispered, "We found it by the car, Jill. You must have dropped it when you burst the balloons."

Titus added, "And you got frosting on your sleeve when you messed with the cake."

Sarah-Jane looked up at the clock. By now Jerry and his groomsmen would be in Grandpa's study. The church was filling up fast. In just fifteen minutes the wedding would start.

"*Please*, Jill!" said Sarah-Jane, after another group of guests went by. "We need the ring NOW! We know you must have it!"

Jill scowled at them. "And I suppose you little tattletales are going to tell on me?"

"We don't want to *tell* on you," said Timothy. "All we want is the ring. Jerry is *so worried* about it!"

To their surprise, tears came to Jill's eyes. "I

36

didn't *mean* to keep it. I was going to pretend to find it—and then give it back. But I was still mad. And it kept getting later and later.'' Jill blinked hard and handed out some more programs.

Titus asked, ''Why did you take the ring in the first place? What are you so mad about?''

''Because I hate this stupid wedding,'' said Jill. ''Nobody cares about me. Christina doesn't like me. That's why she didn't ask me to be a bridesmaid.''

Sarah-Jane said, ''Jill, you have some things

mixed up! Christina probably has lots of girl relatives who had to be bridesmaids. She gave you this job *because* she likes you."

Sarah-Jane looked around desperately. The bridesmaids had come out of the side room. Behind them the cousins and Jill could see Christina. She looked very beautiful and very happy.

"Come on, Jill," said Sarah-Jane. "Christina doesn't know about the ring. Think how she'll *feel* if Jerry doesn't have it for her at the wedding!"

Quickly Jill opened her little purse and took out the ring. She passed it into Sarah-Jane's hand as if she were playing Button, Button, Who's Got the Button?

No one saw.

"Go!" Jill whispered urgently. "Hurry! Please!"

9

NO TIME TO EXPLAIN

There was no time to go outside and around to get to Grandpa's study. So the cousins had to cut through the sanctuary.

They walked quickly and quietly down the side aisle.

They tried not to run.

They tried not to notice the people who stared at them curiously.

They slipped out of the side door. And they ran right into Grandpa coming out of his study with Jerry and Bob and the groomsmen.

"The ring!" whispered Sarah-Jane.

"No time to explain!" said Titus.

"It's a l-o-n-g story!" said Timothy.

The three cousins slipped back through the door. They tiptoed quickly up the aisle and slid into the pew beside their grandmother.

She gave them a puzzled smile. But again there was no time to explain.

The flower girl was coming down the aisle. The wedding had started.

10
HAPPILY EVER AFTER

It was a beautiful wedding. It was a wonderful wedding. It was the best wedding Timothy, Titus, and Sarah-Jane had ever seen.

They listened very seriously as Jerry and Christina made their promises to each other and to God.

And they heaved a sigh of relief when Jerry put the ring on Christina's finger.

The reception was wonderful, too. Each cousin got a piece of cake with a big, sugary flower on it. And all the flowers were the same size.

"Hey, look over there," Titus said.

Across the room, Christina and Jerry, Grandma and Grandpa, and Jill were all talking quietly together.

"Jill must have told on herself," said Sarah-

Jane. "I think she's telling Christina and Jerry that she's sorry for all she did."

"I'm sure they'll forgive her," said Timothy.

And of course, they did. In fact, later, when Christina turned to toss the bouquet, she aimed it right to where Jill was standing. And Jill caught it with a great, big smile.

Then it was time for the bride and groom to drive away in their decorated car.

But before they did, they called Timothy, Titus, and Sarah-Jane over to them. "We sure do appreciate all you've done for us," said Jerry.

"Oh, yes," said Christina. "What would we have done without you?"

Christina hugged Sarah-Jane tight. Jerry shook hands with Timothy and Titus.

The cousins waved and waved until the car was out of sight.

"Whew!" said Sarah-Jane with a laugh. "What a day! You guys were right. Weddings are *weird*."

Timothy and Titus stared at her. "Are you kidding? Weddings are WONDERFUL!"

The End

THE TEN COMMANDMENTS MYSTERIES

When Timothy, Titus, and Sarah-Jane, the three cousins, get together the most ordinary events turn into mysteries. So they've formed the T.C.D.C. (That's the Three Cousins Detective Club.)

And while the three cousins are solving mysteries, they're also learning about the Ten Commandments and living God's way.

You'll want to solve all ten mysteries along with Sarah-Jane, Ti, and Tim:

The Mystery of the Laughing Cat—"You shall not steal." *Someone stole rare coins. Can the cousins find the thief?*

The Mystery of the Messed-up Wedding—"You shall not commit adultery." *Can the cousins find the missing wedding ring?*

The Mystery of the Gravestone Riddle—"You shall not murder." *Can the cousins solve a 100-year-old murder case?*

The Mystery of the Carousel Horse—"You shall not covet." *Why does the stranger want an old, wooden horse?*

The Mystery of the Vanishing Present—"Remember the Sabbath day and keep it holy." *Can the cousins figure out who has Grandpa's missing birthday gift?*

The Mystery of the Silver Dolphin—"You shall not give false testimony." *Who's telling the truth—and who's lying?*

The Mystery of the Tattletale Parrot—"You shall not misuse the name of the Lord your God." *What will the beautiful green parrot say next?*

The Mystery of the Second Map—"You shall have no other gods before me." *Can the cousins discover who dropped the strange map?*

The Mystery of the Double Trouble—"Honor your father and your mother." *How could Timothy be in two places at once?*

The Mystery of the Silent Idol—"You shall not make for yourself an idol." *If the idol could speak, what would it tell the cousins?*

Available at your local Christian bookstore.

David C. Cook Publishing Co., Elgin, IL 60120

SHOELACES AND BRUSSELS SPROUTS

One little lie, but BIG trouble!

When Alex lies to her mom about losing her shoelaces, it doesn't seem like a big deal. But how do you replace special baseball laces when you don't have any money and you're not allowed to go to the store alone? A big softball game is coming up, and Alex knows the coach won't let her pitch in shoes without laces—or in cowboy boots!

Every kid gets into the predicaments that Alex does—ones that start out small and mushroom. Readers will learn from Alex's mistakes and understand that they have the same sources of help that she turns to: A God who loves them and wants to help them, and parents who understand.

Other books in the Alex Series . . .

2 *French Fry Forgiveness*—Sometimes making friends is harder than making enemies.

3 *Hot Chocolate Friendship*—Is winning first place as important to Alex as being a friend?

4 *Peanut Butter and Jelly Secrets*—Obeying her parents (even in little things) beats the awful results of disobeying.

Available at your local Christian bookstore.

David C. Cook Publishing Co.
850 N. Grove Ave.
Elgin, IL 60120

Chariot Books